Our family got a
DIVORCE

*By
Carolyn E.
Phillips*

A Division of G/L Publications
Glendale, California, U.S.A.

The foreign language publishing of all Regal books is under the direction of *Gospel Literature International* (GLINT), a missionary assistance organization founded in 1961 by Dr. Henrietta C. Mears. Each year *Gospel Literature International* provides financial and technical help for the adaptation, translation and publishing of books and Bible study materials in more than 85 languages for millions of people worldwide.

For more information you are invited to write to *Gospel Literature International*, Glendale, California 91204.

Published by Regal Books Division, G/L Publications
Glendale, California 91209
Printed in U.S.A.

Library of Congress Catalog Card No. 78-74006
ISBN 0-8307-0677-1

To my two favorite young people — Rob and Cara

Thank you for your love, patience and your
sense of humor. Most of all thanks for sharing
it with me. We've been through a lot together, you
and me and God. And He's still growing us, I can tell
when I look at you.

CONTENTS

PREFACE

Our family got a divorce in 1972 and
we began to learn. We learned about
sad and lonely feelings. We learned how
to care. We cried and we laughed—
sometimes together, sometimes alone.

We all changed. Most of the change
was good. I wrote this book because I
wanted other divorced families to know
that the sad things do go away. And
while they are going, we *can* become
stronger, more caring people. We *can*
learn to understand other people's
feelings better *because* we got divorced.

I want you to know that our children,
Rob and Cara, were scared, hurt and
angry about our divorce. But I especially
want you to know that Jesus Christ fills
up the angry, hurt and scared places
with His special love and understanding.

Rob and Cara are two happily growing-up people now.

This book is a story about divorce. It is a story of a boy named Chip, his sister, his Gram, his friends *and* his mom and dad. Because nobody gets divorced alone.

Carolyn E. Phillips

Yorba Linda, California

A LETTER TO MOMS AND DADS

My children and I have known the pain of divorce. I want to help you and your child find understanding and comfort from what we have learned. That's why I've written Chip's story.

Within the pages of this book I hope

that Chip will provide opportunities for you and your child to talk honestly about your feelings—all of them. As we experience some of the changes divorce causes, we need to share with someone. Divorce is a crushing thing to us who are adults. It can be terrifying to our children. We need to learn to accept our feelings and share them.

Adjusting to any major change in life (e.g., divorce, death, a job change, moving) takes us through several major phases. Each of us sets our own pace in moving through these steps. We may even experience some of these stages several times.

The first phase for each of us is *denial,* a period of rejecting or ignoring the "facts" in our life. Once we are ready to admit what our circumstances really are, a state of *anger* takes over. Admitting to reality, we sometimes experience a feeling of deep-seated rage over what is happening to us. The third phase is a time of *bargaining*—dealing with God or someone who is in control where we are not. In this phase we attempt to exchange something we are willing to give up for what we want to keep.

Once we realize that *denying,* being *angry* and *bargaining* don't change

11

things, there comes a period of
depression when things seem larger than
life. We feel overwhelmed. We feel we
can't cope. Finally, when we recognize
that life can and will go on we are free
to move into the final and only restful
phase. We enter into *acceptance,* where
we begin learning to live with the
changes in our life.

In this book, Chip walks through
problems that most children face when
their parents divorce. He stumbles
through each of the phases we've just
discussed. *Our Family Got a Divorce* is
designed to help children make the
adjustments they need to make to accept

their new situation. I hope this book will provide a few answers if *you* are hurting from divorce. But most of all I want you to discover that with Jesus Christ, our unfailing, unchanging, special Friend, there is always hope.

I encourage you to talk with your children. Listen to what they say. Help them put their feelings into words. They need to talk with someone who is sensitive and caring, who will help them clarify and define their feelings.

We all hope our children will be hurt as little as possible by divorce. We long for them to develop confident, positive attitudes as they face the responsibilities of living life. Building an environment where these attitudes can flourish is difficult at best. It never just "happens." It needs to be a conscious part of our daily routine.

Here are some suggestions that may help you encourage the kind of growth you want in your children.

If your child asks you how mom or dad feels or what he or she is doing, encourage him to ask the other parent himself. You cannot answer for someone else. Eliminate that unnecessary strain on yourself. Guard against making excuses for the absent parent or creating wonderful fantasies your child wants to

hear by making the parent a super hero.
Above all, avoid tearing down qualities
the other parent possesses because you
are angry or hurt.

*If your children hear cruel or unkind
things about you,* be confident that they
know you. Tell them how you feel. You
might say: "Sometimes when people are
angry they say unkind things about
someone else. You and I know each
other better than anybody else. That
means you can tell when someone is
saying what is true. If you're not sure,
you can come and ask me. We can talk
about things anytime."

If your children have questions, be

willing to answer them. Bedtime is usually a comfortable time for them to talk. Some special "all alone times" with mom or dad in secure surroundings can help build and maintain a solid relationship between you.

Give truthful answers to their questions. *Details* are seldom necessary but honesty always is. Honesty builds trust. Talk about *your* feelings. For instance, "I feel very lonely sometimes too. But I have Jesus and I have you, and that's pretty special."

If your former mate remarries and the new spouse wants your children to call her/him "Mom" or "Dad," don't feel

16

threatened. Nothing changes the fact
that *you* are their parent, and always
will be. And no one knows that better
than your children. Reassure them often
of your love.

Regardless of whether or not you
remarry, *help your children understand
that their absent parent is still "Mom"
or "Dad."* (Remember, a poor mate can
be a great parent.) Encourage children
to build a relationship with that parent
whenever possible. It will strengthen
your own relationship with them.

*Tell your children some of the
problems and needs you are giving to
God.* Then, as He responds to you,

17

share the answers with them too. (We share the needs to share the blessings!) There is a direct relationship between our children seeing us actively trust God with our needs and their trusting Him with their own needs. (Most of us learn best by example.)

Be willing to say "I was wrong." Parents weren't designed to be perfect. But we can be living object lessons of how He works in human lives and events when we let Him. If, for instance, you lose your temper, ask your children's forgiveness. This will help them know you are genuine and approachable. Children need to know

we're real people who make mistakes the
same as they do. We need to let them
see God's changing power in *our* lives.

*Keep thanking God for His love and
blessings even when they are hard to see.*
He's "growing us"—all of us—and
growing is usually painful. Make
trusting God a habit and teach it to your
children.

Learn to be a good listener. You will
see their feelings change in time. And
being a good listener is a very special
skill.

I hope *Our Family Got a Divorce* will
be helpful in keeping you and your
children talking and listening to each

other. And I pray the Lord will bless you as you work through this growing experience, together in His love, one day at a time.

If you have comments, questions and/or suggestions I would enjoy hearing from you. Write to me in care of Regal Books, 110 W. Broadway, Glendale, California 91204.

A NOTE FROM CHIP

Hi. I'm Chip. I'm a kid like you. I have a super tough bike. I can do wheelies all the way to the corner.

I have a little sister we call Sis. She's not too bad for a girl, even if she does follow me around. She likes to play football with me and the guys. One time we let her play. She made a touchdown—for the other team.

And I bet you'll like my gram. She's pretty neat. She's kinda old, 43 or something. But she likes us kids around.

Her cookie jar is always full when we get there—but not when we leave.

Anyway, here's my story about what happened in our family.

Oh, I almost forgot. You gotta meet my mom and dad too. Dad teaches big

kids at the high school by the park. He tells 'em how to do their math and stuff. And in the afternoons he coaches the new kids' basketball team. Sometimes I watch 'em practicing. I'm gonna be a basketball player—soon as I get taller.

And this is Mom. I like her a lot. She used to be home all the time, but now she's got a job working with sick people in a doctor's office. I liked it best when she was just my mom. I guess sometimes things just can't be the way we want 'em to be. Guess we just gotta get used to the new stuff then. And that's not easy.

Chapter 1

BAD NEWS!

I like being me. I like my bike and you know what's neat? I can do wheelies. Yeah, just about everything is great. Except one day when just about everything went bad.

I heard Mom call me. When I got into the house Mom and Dad were sitting there with Sis and they looked real serious.

I tried hard to remember if I did something to get in trouble for. I couldn't remember anything. But nobody was smiling even a little bit. Something was awful wrong.

"Kids," Dad said, "people who live together try to get along. When they don't agree on something they try to make up a new way to make everybody happy.

"But even though they try very hard, sometimes there are problems they just can't find answers to.

"Your mom and I love both of you very, very much. That will never change. But things with Mom and me *have* changed. We have some very hard problems we can't work out. So we think it will be better for all of us if we don't live together."

Mom pulled Sis on her lap. I wished I wasn't so big 'cause I wanted to be on somebody's lap too. I was scared.

Then Mom said, "You'll still get to see Daddy. He loves you just as much as ever. But he has another place to live, very close to our house. You'll still see him a lot."

"But, Dad," I asked, "when will you come back and live with us?"

"I'm not going to move back, son. Your mom and I are getting a divorce."

"Divorce?" I said, "I don't know what that means, but if you're not gonna live here on account of a divorce, I don't want one."

Dad put his arm around me. It made me cry. I was so scared I couldn't help it. He said, "Chip, divorce is when people who are married get a paper that says they're not married anymore. But there will never be any papers that can make your mom or me not love you and Sis anymore."

"You still gonna be my dad? Even if you don't live here with me?"

"You bet I am. I'll always be your dad. Nothing can change that—ever!"

Dad got quiet for a minute, then he hugged me again and said, "I want you to do something for me. I want you to stop trying to figure out tomorrow before it gets here. Take one day at a time. You won't always feel the way you do right now. I know you must be very sad and probably scared. But those feelings are going to change."

Mom said, "It's going to take time, honey. We all need time to get used to the new things in our lives." Mom didn't talk anymore. I could tell she was trying not to cry.

Dad asked, "Will you try to take one day at a time? For me?"

"I'll try, Dad," I said, "but I wish you'd just stay here with us instead."

"We'll see each other a whole lot, I promise. But I can't stay. Mom and I have thought and thought, and really prayed about what to do, and we think this will be the best for all of us."

"Oh, Dad," I said, "I'm gonna miss you so much." I hugged my dad real tight. He didn't answer me. I could tell he was crying too.

Chapter 2

MY FAULT?

I heard Dad's car start up outside. I kicked the covers off and ran to my window. Dad was putting his suitcase in the trunk. Then he got in the car, turned on the lights and backed out of the driveway. He was gone.

I got back in bed and pulled the covers up under my chin. Max stuck his nose next to my face. It felt wet and cold. I rolled over and put my arm around his big shaggy neck. "I guess Mom and Dad really are gonna get divorced. I can't believe it, Max. If it's the 'best thing' like Dad said, how come I feel so crummy?"

The next day was Saturday. I got my tennis shoes on and sort of made my bed. Then Max raced me downstairs but I didn't race him this time. I didn't feel like running.

After breakfast I told Mom, "I'm gonna go to Gram's house." My gram likes to listen to me and I like the way she makes me feel. Gram loves Jesus so much I feel like He's right in the room when she talks. I think He's her best Friend.

I knocked on the door and Gram opened it up. She pretended she was surprised to see me. I go to her house every Saturday and she always plays like she's surprised.

We talked about some stuff and we walked around in her big old yard. Then we decided we'd make some cookies. While we were mixing up the stuff for cookies I asked Gram, "How come my dad left?"

Gram stopped stirring the flour and butter. She looked at me for a minute, then she started turning her big wooden spoon again. "Chip," Gram said, "grown-up problems are hard to understand, even for grown-ups. Your mom and dad are doing the best they can to solve the problems they have."

I asked, "Did Dad leave because I wasn't being good enough? I been thinkin' about it all morning. Maybe if I was REAL good they wouldn't get a divorce."

"Other children sometimes feel just like you do, Chip. They sort of feel like if they were never bad their parents wouldn't argue or get divorced. Kids can't solve grown-up problems, no matter how good they are. Your dad would never leave because you were naughty. You didn't make him leave and you can't make him come back, no matter how much you want to. You have to let your parents do what they think is best."

"But, Gram, I don't like it with Dad gone. I miss him so bad. And he just left last night."

"Lonely feelings are hard for everybody, honey. Just remember that you have a special Friend who is always

34

with you. He *never* leaves you alone. He promised."

"You mean Jesus, Gram?"

"That's right. Jesus is right here *all* the time and He promised to be your Friend. Nothing can change that, ever!"

Chapter 3

FOLKS HAVE FEELINGS

Max and me were playing catch in our backyard, and I was thinking a lot about what Gram said. It felt better knowing Jesus was still around too.

Pretty soon I heard something that sounded like somebody crying. I threw the ball to Max and went in the house. When I opened Mom's door she was sitting on her bed with tears on her face.

I walked over to her and patted her arm. Mom kinda wiped her eyes and put her arms around me.

I hugged her and said, "What's the matter, Mom? How come you're crying?"

She patted me a little bit and said, "I just feel bad about our divorce sometimes, honey."

"But, Mom, Gram says our friend Jesus is here *all* the time. He doesn't ever go away from us."

"You know, Chip, sometimes I think about how sad I feel instead of thinking about Jesus and how much He loves us. You just made me remember Him right now. And I don't feel so sad anymore. You're a real helper and a brave boy."

"I'm not brave, Mom. I'm scared a whole lot."

"Honey, somebody who's brave does what he has to do while he IS still scared. There's no reason to be brave if you're not scared."

"I never thought about that before. All I know is I love you, Mom. I wish you wouldn't be sad."

"Thank you for loving me, Chip, and thanks for reminding me how much Jesus loves me."

Chapter 4

I'LL FIX IT, MOM

A couple days later I came home from school. I ran into the kitchen and put my lunch box on the sink. Mom was sitting at the table with a cup of coffee. She was sad again, I could tell.

"Do you want some cookies, Mom?" I asked. "I got three big ones for me."

"No thanks."

"Can we go to the park with Max? He

wants to go, he really wants to."

Mom looked up, "Not today, Chip. I don't feel like going to the park."

I tried to make Mom feel better, but she just stayed sad. I got feeling pretty sad myself and just stopped talking. It was awful quiet. I couldn't make Mom feel better and I didn't like that.

Finally I said, "I'm gonna take Max over to Gram's."

"OK. Be back to do your chores."

Gram and I talked about being sad and she said, "Everybody feels sad sometimes."

"But, Gram, I don't like it when Mom is sad. I like her to be happy. I like when she sings."

"Sometimes, Chip, we need to feel sad for a while. Feeling sad helps us get used to unhappy changes in our lives. And

feeling better is something we all do for ourselves. But, I think there is something you can do that will help your mom."

"Like what, Gram? What can I do?"

"Love her, Chip."

That was a funny thing for Gram to say.

"But I do love her and she knows I do, Gram."

"You're right. She knows that you love her. But sometimes we have to get our love out where people can see it. We can't just tell them about it all the time. What we *do* speaks louder than what we say."

"You mean, when I do stuff at home I'm telling Mom I love her?"

"Yes. You're saying it without words. Your mom knows you love her. But when she's feeling sad, if you do something very special—like clean your room without being asked to or wash the dishes to surprise her—then she can see that you love her."

All the way home I thought about what Gram said. I thought about saying and doing. And I decided to try to say "I love you" at least one time every day without using words.

Chapter 5

HIDING FROM FRIENDS

Saturday when I went to the park, my best friend Pete was there.

"Hey, Chip," he hollered. "We're playin' ball with our dads this afternoon. You comin' ?"

I told him, "Nah, who wants to play in a dumb old ball game anyway? *My* dad's got important things to do, too important to be playin' ball all day."

45

Pete looked surprised. All he said was, "OK. See ya later, huh?"

"Yeah, see ya."

I felt bad for what I said. I was sort of mad at Pete. But what really made me mad was that Dad wasn't around to play ball with me anymore. I felt funny inside, I didn't tell Pete anything. I just hollered at him instead.

I walked in the house and slammed the door.

Mom looked up and said, "Somebody sounds angry."

"I'm mad at Pete."

"How come?"

I tried to make it sound like Mom oughta be mad at him too. But I didn't have any good reasons. "I don't know why I'm mad at Pete. He asked me and Dad to play ball with them at the park.

I really am mad at him—but I don't know why."

"Does Pete know Dad's gone?" Mom asked.

"I didn't tell anybody." My face got hot.

"Honey," Mom said. "I think you'd feel better if some of your friends knew about our divorce."

"But Mom, I don't want 'em thinking I'm weird or feeling sorry for me or something. I'm scared they won't be my friends anymore."

"Chip, real friends love us for what we are. We don't need to pretend with real friends. I think Pete would understand. But you have to give him a chance.

"And don't forget, Chip, we have one Friend who is closer to us than anybody else. Remember what you told me before? That day I was feeling sad?"

"I guess you're right, Mom, I *should* tell Pete. And if he doesn't understand, I still have Jesus for my Friend.

"I gotta go to Gram's, Mom, but I'll be back on time."

Chapter 6

I'M MAD!

Gram opened her door and said, "Well, hello, there young man. What a nice surprise. Come in. Come in." (Isn't she neat?)

We had some warm cookies and milk in Gram's big yellow kitchen. "Gram," I said, "I was mean to my friend, Pete, today. He asked if me and Dad were going to be at the ball game, and I got mad at him."

Gram smiled a little bit and asked, "Do you remember when you hit your thumb with a hammer? How did it feel when you bumped it again?"

"It *really* hurt, " I said. "It was already sore."

"That's just the way our feelings are inside us, Chip. When we feel bad about something, even little things can make us very angry. They make us hurt all over again."

"You mean, I was mad at Pete 'cause Dad moved away? I don't understand that!"

Gram said, "Understanding our feelings is hard to do. It hurts to have to think about sad feelings. Sometimes I'll bet you feel like you're the only kid who feels like you do."

"How'd you know that, Gram?"

" 'Cause everybody feels that way when they hurt, Chip. Even grown-ups. That's why we do things like getting mad at friends. Do you suppose you could make Pete feel better?"

"Well, I could tell him I'm sorry. And I guess I should tell him about the divorce. Do you think he'll understand?"

"Well, Chip, real friends try to understand."

Chapter 7

GOOD FRIENDS

On my way home I stopped by Pete's house. He was sitting on his front porch. "Hey, Pete!"

He looked up, "Oh, hi."

I asked, "Wanna play some catch?"

"I guess so." He picked up his ball and mitt.

We tossed the ball back and forth but nobody talked. I wanted to tell Pete about being sorry. I wanted to tell him about Dad being gone but I was scared. In my head I prayed, "Jesus, I'm scared. What if I tell Pete I'm sorry and he stays mad at me? I want him to be my friend."

Finally I said, "Pete, I'm sorry I got mad at you."

And he said, "Aw, it's OK."

In my head I prayed real quick, "Thanks, Jesus." Boy! Did I feel better!

He threw the ball back again and I said, "My dad moved away. They're getting divorced."

Pete caught the ball and held it a minute, "That's the pits." He threw the ball back. "You know Terrie? The new girl in our class? Her mom and dad are getting divorced. That's how come she moved here. I'm sure glad my mom and dad aren't splitting up. I wouldn't like it."

"It's the pits alright," I said. "Sometimes at night I think maybe it's just a bad dream. I wish it was."

We played ball and talked a while. Then I had to go. I ran all the way home. I felt lots better inside. Pete and me were OK. That's real important 'cause Pete's my very best friend. It's neat to know he cares how I feel. I care how he feels about stuff too. Gram says that's how to be a friend.

I think I know what the verse I had to learn at Sunday School this week means now—a man who wants friends has to be friendly. Sometimes taking the first step is the hardest part.

Chapter 8

HOPING DAD HOME

The next day Dad was coming. I watched for his car from my window. When he pulled into the driveway I ran for the stairs. I beat Max to the bottom and opened the door before Dad could even ring the bell. Just for a second it seemed almost funny to see him again. He hugged me and Sis and we ran out to the car. I turned

59

around to say good-bye to Mom. She looked all alone. I said, "Mom, you come too."

"Oh, I don't think so, honey. You go have a good time and I'll see you later."

It seemed funny to leave without Mom.

When we got in the car I got to sit next to Dad. I started thinking about some stuff—like what if they liked each other again. Wouldn't it be neat if they got back together? I got real excited about Dad coming home—maybe.

"Dad," I said, "you like Mom again? You were real nice at the house. Does that mean you like her again?"

Dad looked at me and then looked back at the road. "Chip, I am always going to try to be nice to your mother, but that doesn't mean anything's changed between us. I'm not coming home, son."

It was so hard to hear Dad say those things. I want him to love Mom again. I wish I could make him love her. I don't like things the way they are.

Chapter 9

MAKE IT LIKE IT WAS

A couple days later I was still feeling unhappy, and I was just sitting in my room. My sister came in and said, "Chip, I broke my pencil. Can I use one of yours?"

All of a sudden I was mad, like when I was mad at Pete. "No, you can't. I need 'em. *All* of 'em. You'd just break it anyway. Go away! Leave me alone!"

Sis looked real surprised and then kinda sad. She shut my door and went away. I felt awful. I wouldn't have felt so bad if she'd yelled back at me or something. I really needed somebody to talk to. "Jesus, I don't know why I get so mad at people. I don't want to do it. My gram says it's 'cause I'm mad about our divorce.

"Well—I AM! I want things how they used to be. I want my dad here with me. I miss him so much. I promise I'll never give Sis a bad time again, not ever! if you'll just bring Dad back. I'll be so good you won't even know it's me. Please, Jesus, make it like it was."

I went to bed that night and I wondered if maybe God was mad at me and that was why we were getting a divorce. Maybe it's because I haven't been good. I was thinking about that when Mom came in to say good night.

"Mom, does God punish people when they're bad?"

"Honey, God loves us very much and never does anything to 'get us.' It makes Him sad to see us disobey, and He wants to hear us ask Him to forgive us when we do, but He loves us always. Why did you ask me that?"

" 'Cause I've been praying and praying about something real important and nothing happens. I thought maybe it might be 'cause I haven't been very good. If He's not punishing me how come He doesn't answer my prayer?"

Mom sat down on my bed. "Chip, I want you to remember something. Jesus ALWAYS answers your prayers. Sometimes He says yes. Other times He says wait a while. And sometimes He has to say no. That's because He loves us. Honey, Jesus loves you more than you can imagine. And when He says no to you it's because He's got a very special reason. That's when we really need to trust Him because He's God, and He always knows what's best."

Chapter 10

VISITING DAY

The next time Dad came for me and Sis he took us to the fair. We went on all the rides and saw *everything*. We ate popcorn and hot dogs, and Sis got cotton candy in her hair. Dad won some big stuffed dogs for us. And we stayed out very late. We had a great time.

Mom helped us get ready for bed and

before she turned out my light I told her what a great time we had.

"I'm glad you did, honey."

"I really like being with Dad, but . . . I miss you."

Mom said, "That must be hard for you, Chip. I think I would feel the very same."

After the light was out and Mom left, I cried just a little. "It's not fair, Jesus. It's not fair at all. I want my dad home. I know he still loves me but I want him here. I miss him so much."

Chapter 11

SOMETIMES LOVE SAYS NO

The next night, really early, Mom said I had to take a bath and get to bed. "But it's early," I argued. "I'm too big to go to bed so early."

"You were out very late last night and you have school tomorrow. It won't be early when you finish taking your bath."

I slammed the bathroom door behind me and turned the water on to fill the tub. "She's just mad 'cause we had a good time with Dad last night. Dad wouldn't make me go to bed so early if I was living with him, I'll bet. He understands how a guy feels about things. He doesn't make me do dumb things I don't like. And he takes me neat places and buys great stuff for me. I get just about anything I want when I'm with him. Mom's changed a lot. She isn't fun anymore."

Mom opened the bathroom door. I jumped 'cause I thought she was gonna swat me for slamming the door like I did. "Don't forget to wash behind your ears, and make it a quick bath." Mom closed the door again and I got in the tub real quick.

I finished taking my bath and got into bed. I tried to stay awake all night just to show Mom. I didn't do so good. I went to sleep anyway.

After school I stopped by Gram's

'cause I promised to help work in her garden. I told her about going to the fair and all about how much fun it was. She asked lots of questions. She said she was glad we had such a good time.

"Gram, if we had a good time with Dad would that make Mom mad?"

"What makes you think that might make her angry?"

"Well, last night she was real grumpy. I mean, she made me take a bath and go to bed and it was too early. I'm too big to go to bed that early."

"Oh, I see," Gram said. She pulled her gardening gloves up higher and finished weeding another row of red flowers.

"Dad does all kinds of great stuff when we're with him. He takes us neat places, and buys us presents and hardly ever says no."

"Chip, when parents say no," Gram said, "they don't do it to be mean. They say no because they love us. Your dad used to say no lots more before he moved away—remember? Since you only see him once in a while now he can sort of let things go a little. The parent you're living with can't do that. Saying no is part of saying I love you. That's called responsibility. That's called love."

Chapter 12

THE EMPTY HOUSE

After school one day I was walking home. Mom wasn't going to be there 'cause she's got a job now. It's neat to have my own house key and Sis likes the lady she stays with too. But it's not the same as having Mom home. The house is kinda . . . well, cold and sort of empty.

I opened the back door and put my

stuff down on the counter. There was a note for me on the refrigerator. Here's what it said:

"Hi, Chip. I miss being home with you when you get there. I'm so glad Jesus gave you to me. Thank you for learning new ways with me. I love you, Mom.

P.S. Have some cookies. Gram sent them for you and Sis."

The whole house was warm after I read Mom's note. It was *almost* as good as having her there. She cares how I feel, even while she's away at work.

I wonder if she likes her job. I liked it better when she was home. I never even asked how she feels. Sometimes I forget—grown-ups have feelings too.

Chapter 13

A NEW LADY

One of the times Dad came to get Sis and me he said he wanted us to meet somebody. We drove for a while and then stopped at a house. When we rang the bell a lady opened the door and was real happy to see us. She got her coat and we all got into Dad's car.

Sis and I had to sit in the back seat 'cause the lady sat next to Dad. She sat

real close like Mom used to. And they held hands and talked real quiet sometimes.

"Oh, Jesus," I prayed in my heart, "isn't Dad ever gonna love my mom again?"

I was at Gram's house later and I told her about the lady. "Oh, Gram, I don't like that lady. She's nice and all that stuff, but . . . well, she's not Mom. Dad's never coming home now, I just know it! I gotta do something!"

"Come over here and sit beside me," Gram said. "Do you trust Jesus?"

"What do you mean, Gram?"

"I mean do you believe with all your heart that Jesus knows and cares about what's happening in your life right now? Do you believe that He will do what is best for you?"

"Sure," I said. "I've been asking Him to make Dad come back, but now there's this lady . . ."

"That's just what I mean, honey," Gram said. "If you really trust Jesus let Him do things HIS WAY, not your way. Even when we don't understand what His way is, when it looks like everything is wrong, we have to remember that Jesus is still in control. Nothing takes Him by surprise. We have to remind ourselves that He loves us and He is working in our lives *all* the time."

"I know He loves me, Gram. But I love my dad and I want him to come home. I guess God could have a different plan, couldn't He? I know He really loves me. Maybe I should try to do it His way, for a change."

Chapter 14

BEING HONEST

Mom was going through the mail after supper one evening. "Chip, come here for a minute."

I walked over to her at the table. She had a letter in her hand. "I just got this letter from your school. It says you're not doing as well as you should be. What's happening to your schoolwork, honey?"

"I don't know."

"Chip, I know you've been upset over the divorce and my new job. Is that making it hard for you to study?"

Mom looked real worried. I felt so bad. I was having a real hard time keeping my mind on stuff at school sometimes. But I said, "Aw, no, Mom. Your old divorce doesn't bother me anymore. Not even a little bit. Nothing's wrong. I think maybe Bryan, the kid who sits next to me, talks too much. My next report card will be better. You'll see."

Nobody at school was talking too much. But I didn't want to tell Mom how I really felt about things now. I didn't want to make her feel worse.

I thought a "little white lie" would make everybody happier. But it made me feel real bad. I felt so far away from my mom. I didn't tell her the truth.

I went to bed that night, but I couldn't sleep. I laid on my back and stared at the ceiling, then I curled up in a ball—but I couldn't get comfortable. Mom was folding clothes in the kitchen when I went back downstairs.

"I can't sleep, Mom. I hafta tell you something."

"OK, honey. What is it?"

"I didn't tell you the truth tonight. I *do* feel bad about our divorce. And I don't like Dad with that lady. I feel so bad."

Mom hugged me real tight and I guess I cried a little bit.

"Honey," Mom said, "sometimes I still feel pretty awful myself. But Jesus has promised He'll always be with us. We can be strong with HIS strength when ours is all gone.

"And, you know what, Chip, I'm having some days now and then when I don't feel so bad. It isn't easy. But living one day at a time makes it easier when we know Jesus is right beside us every single minute. Someday everything's going to be different."

"I'm sorry I didn't tell you the truth before. I didn't want you to know how I was feeling 'cause I didn't want you to feel bad."

"Honey, I'm glad you thought about my feelings. But I want you to remember something. God is working in my life at the *same time* He's working in yours. If you have hurting feelings you tell me and we'll trust God together to help us both with the hurt. OK?"

"OK, Mom. I promise. I feel better now. I'm glad I have you to share with. It's funny too, 'cause you can't *change* how I feel. But it's neat to tell you how I feel."

"Jesus said we should help each other with heavy things. Do you suppose sharing makes a heavy load a little lighter because there's two of us to carry it?"

"Yeah, helping makes things easier. I love you, Mom."

"And I love you too, Chip."

Chapter 15

IT'S OK TO CRY

I felt kinda funny next morning when I went downstairs for breakfast. I was wishing I hadn't cried last night, 'specially in front of my mom.

Mom asked me, "Are you alright?"

"Yeah," I said, "I just feel . . . well, kinda dumb."

"What makes you feel like that?"

"Aw, Mom, when we were talking last night I—well, I cried. Big kids like me aren't supposed to cry anymore. 'Specially boys! I feel like a regular sissy."

"Chip, even big kids like you are allowed to feel sad. Even moms and dads do sometimes. Crying helps get rid of some of the sad feelings and bad feelings inside us. When we don't cry, all those sad and bad feelings stay inside getting bigger and bigger. Crying makes us feel better and think better, then we can do a better job of being us. It's OK to cry."

Mom sat down at the table with me and said, "Honey, feelings are like color in a picture. Without feelings everything is plain old black and white. But feelings make the world full of color."

"I like color best."

"Chip."

"Yeah, Mom?"
"You know what I remembered?"
"What, Mom?"
"Jesus cried."

Chapter 16

SOMEBODY WHO KNOWS

Sunday morning I was walking up the church steps. Somebody hollered, "Hi, Chip!"

I turned around. It was the new girl, Terrie. "Oh, hi. I didn't know you came to our church."

She said, "We just started coming last week. We just moved here."

I asked her, "How come you moved in

the middle of the school year? Isn't it hard to catch up?"

"Yeah," she said, "but my mom and dad got divorced. So we had to move."

"Your parents are divorced?"

"Yeah," Terrie answered.

"We're getting divorced too," I told her.

She said, "It's the pits, isn't it?"

"It sure is," I said.

Terrie said, "I don't get to see my mom very much anymore since she left. But Dad and me, we're doing OK. And I guess there's some good stuff too."

"Good stuff?" I asked. "Like what?"

Terrie grinned like she knew a big secret, "Well, like first I was scared all the time. Then I started telling Jesus how scared I was. And after a while I wasn't scared so much anymore."

"Hey, you sound like my gram. She knows Jesus really good. I think He's her best Friend."

"Is Jesus your best friend, Chip?"

"I want Him to be. I talk to Him a lot. I'm going to ask Him to help me find some good stuff in our divorce. Like you did. I want to know Him better."

"You'll be glad, Chip. He won't let you down."

Chapter 17

JUST LIKE I AM—REALLY?

One Saturday at Gram's I said, "Gram, how can Jesus love me like I am? I do some rotten things sometimes. Don't I have to be pretty good before He can love me a lot?"

Gram said, "Chip, when you've been naughty does your mom or dad pack your suitcase and ask you to leave home?"

That sounded so dumb I laughed, "Of course not, Gram. That's silly."

"Have they ever told you, 'When you can behave yourself then you can be our son'?"

"Gram, Mom and Dad wouldn't ever say that. They LOVE me."

"Jesus loves you too, Chip. Even MORE than your mom and dad do. He knows how bad we can be. But He loves us anyway. He wants us to love Him back. When we do something wrong He wants us to feel sorry for what we've done and ask Him to forgive us. When we ask, He forgives *AND* forgets. Then, with HIS ways He helps us begin to make changes in our lives. Changes that make us become the people He wants us to be.

"Jesus loves us the way we are right

now," Gram continued. "If we wait till we think we're good enough to deserve His love we waste a lot of time. In fact, we never can be good enough to earn His love. That's a special gift to us. He planned it so that we have to accept His love like we do a birthday present. It's a gift, because He loves us, not because we earned it."

"Boy, I never knew Jesus loved me that much before. He's the kind of Friend I want."

"It's pretty special alright," Gram said, "He knows *all* about us before we're born. Nothing we do can make Him stop loving us, ever."

That's *really* love.

Chapter 18

CHANGES

Gram and I were looking at the pictures in her album. "That's you, Chip, when you were only three months old. You were so little you couldn't even feed yourself then."

Then Gram showed me another picture, "Here you are at my house just after your first birthday. You were trying to learn to walk. But you did more falling down than walking."

"Oh, look, Gram," I said after she turned the next page. "Here's one when I was learning to ride my two-wheeler. Look how shaky I was. I can do wheelies now!"

"And remember this one, Chip? You were taking swimming lessons. You didn't think you'd ever learn to swim. Now you swim like a two-legged fish." Gram turned some pages and said, "Our lives are just like these pictures."

I asked, "What do you mean, Gram?"

"Well," she said, "we feel so sad when we're trying to learn something new. We think we'll never be able to learn it. We think we'll always feel dumb and slow. And then one day we look back and discover we're swimming and doing wheelies."

"You mean sometimes we want to give

up, Gram, just because it's hard learning new stuff?"

"That's right, Chip. And wouldn't it be sad if we did give up and quit when it got hard for us?"

"Yeah," I said, "we'd never learn anything new. I couldn't swim or ride my bike."

"That wouldn't be much fun, would it? Learning to do new and hard things makes us grow strong. If we quit when it gets tough we always stay the same, like a baby, all our life."

I thought about what Gram was saying. Then I said, "Gram, our divorce is hard for me. Will it make me stronger?"

"Well," Gram said, "have you seen any changes since your dad left?"

"I *still* wish he lived with us. But

school's going better now. And I'm
learning more about Jesus' love for me.
I didn't know very much about that
before our divorce."

"Then you're seeing some good things
come out of something that's hard for
you, is that right, Chip?"

"Yeah, I guess so, Gram. I never
thought I'd see *any* good stuff in this.
It's scary."

Gram thought a minute then she said,
"Thunderstorms can be pretty scary,
can't they?"

"Yeah, with lightning and all. I don't
like 'em."

"But storms bring rain that makes
flowers grow. I love flowers."

"And Gram, if it didn't rain we'd
never have a rainbow."

Chapter 19

JUST LIKE I AM—REALLY!

ax and me were lying in the grass watching clouds go by. The sky was real blue.

"Jesus," I said, "I've heard about your love since I was just a little kid. And I want to ask you something. Will you be my special Friend forever?

"You love me just the way I am. I don't even LIKE me sometimes. But you LOVE me. And I know you know what's best for me—because you love me.

"I don't think I'll ever like this divorce. But I guess I can make it if you stay with me.

"Thanks for helping me learn, and for making me grow. And, Jesus, thanks for being my very own special Friend."

I wish everybody knew Jesus. He loves all of us. But He can only be a special Friend when we ask Him to be. I hope He's your special Friend, 'cause He loves you—just the way you are.